Mouse Paint

Ellen Stoll Walsh

A Voyager Book
Harcourt Brace & Company
San Diego   New York   London

Requests for permission to make copies of any
part of the work should be mailed to:
Permissions Department, Harcourt Brace & Company,
6277 Sea Harbor Drive, Orlando, Florida 32887-6777.

Library of Congress Cataloging-in-Publication Data
Walsh, Ellen Stoll.
Mouse paint/by Ellen Stoll Walsh.—1st ed.
p.   cm.
Summary: Three white mice discover jars of red, blue, and yellow
paint and explore the world of color.
ISBN 0-15-201051-3
[1. Color—Fiction. 2. Mice—Fiction.] I. Title.
PZ7.W1675Mo 1989 [E]—dc19 88-15694

Special Edition for Trumpet Book Fairs
A B C D E

Printed in Singapore

The illustrations in this book are cut-paper collage.
The text type was set in ITC Modern.
Composition by Photocomposition Center, Harcourt Brace & Company
Printed and bound by Tien Wah Press, Singapore
This book was printed on Leykam recycled paper,
which contains more than 20 percent postconsumer waste and has a
total recycled content of at least 50 percent.
Production supervision by Warren Wallerstein and Rebecca Miller
Designed by Nancy J. Ponichtera

This one's for my mom,
NELL ORUM STOLL JONES

Once there were three white mice on a white
piece of paper.

The cat couldn't find them.

One day, while the cat was asleep, the mice saw
three jars of paint—

one red, one yellow, and one blue.

They thought it was Mouse Paint. They climbed right in.

Then one was red, one was yellow, and one was blue.

They dripped puddles of paint onto the paper.

The puddles looked like fun.

The red mouse stepped into a yellow puddle
and did a little dance.

His red feet stirred the yellow puddle until . . .

"Look," he cried.

"Red feet in a yellow puddle make orange!"

The yellow mouse hopped into a blue puddle.

His feet mixed and stirred and stirred and mixed until . . .

"Look down," said the red mouse and the blue mouse.

"Yellow feet in a blue puddle make green."

Then the blue mouse jumped into a red puddle.

He splashed and mixed and danced until . . .

"Purple!" they all shouted.

"Blue feet in a red puddle make purple!"

But the paint on their fur got sticky and stiff.

So they washed themselves down to a nice soft white

and painted the paper instead. They painted
one part red

and one part yellow

and one part blue.

They mixed red and yellow to paint an orange part,

yellow and blue to paint a green part,

and blue and red to paint a purple part.

But they left some white because of the cat.